MARVEL SUPER HERO SQUAD

HERO UP!

PAUL TOBIN - SCRIPTS AND IDEAS
MARCELO DICHIARA, TODD NAUCK, DARIO BRIZUELA - ART
CHRIS SOTOMAYOR - COLORS
BLAMBOT'S NATE PIEKOS - LETTERS
DICHIARA & SOTOMAYOR - COVER ART
NATHAN COSBY - EDITOR

SUPER SPECIAL THANKS TO COURTNEY LANE,
CHRIS FONDACARO, TOM MARVELLI, PAT MCGRATH,
MARK PANICCIA, RUWAN JAYATILLEKE,
TIM DILLON AND MIKE PASCIULLO

COLLECTION EDITOR: CORY LEVINE
ASSISTANT EDITORS: ALEX STARBUCK & JOHN DENNING
EDITORS, SPECIAL PROJECTS: JENNIFER GRÜNWALD & MARK D. BEAZLEY
SENIOR EDITOR, SPECIAL PROJECTS: JEFF YOUNGQUIST
SENIOR VICE PRESIDENT OF SALES: DAVID GABRIEL
COVER DESIGN: DAYLE CHESLER
INTERIOR DESIGN: NANCY LEE

EDITOR IN CHIEF: JOE QUESADA
PUBLISHER: DAN BUCKLEY
EXECUTIVE PRODUCER: ALAN FINE